MORIAH CHAVIS

Thorns of Winter

A SHORT STORY

MORIAH CHAVIS

Twenty
Hills

Praise

"Chavis spins a fairytale that upends and rebuilds the traditional damsel-in-distress trope. Thorns of Winter is alternately as luscious and as thorny as a castle rose." - Abigail Hobbs, Author of *Scythe and Pen*

"*Thorns of Winter* is a fairy tale full of spells—but the most compelling of them is the story itself, which weaves itself over the reader with high-stakes, explosive action, and characters full of heart and hope. A beautiful tale of courage and the lengths we'll go for the ones we love." - Autumn Krause, Author of *Before the Devil Knows You're Here*

*To my brother, because I forgot you in
the acknowledgments that one time.*

I'm not meant to survive this.

None of the men who are chosen once a year to face the beast in the castle and save the stolen girl are meant to live.

Slay the monster; survive the winter.

One girl taken.

One boy to rescue her.

The problem is, the one who defeats the beast never comes home—and still, the beast returns. The village only knows of the current champion's victory because the winter ebbs to something bearable and eventually ends come March. Every year, the townspeople try some-thing—*someone*—new, but even the winter isn't as unforgiving as the beast inside the castle. It might be a different blade, a new set of armor, or a counterspell.

It never works.

Snow flurries pepper the air as I near the center of the forest. The crumbling, decrepit castle sits half a mile away. Yet it towers over the trees. It's a thing forgotten beneath a tapestry of thorns and vines, all of it weighed down by snow and ice. My lungs ache with every breath as if the debris and dust are clawing inside my chest, but I push forward.

I am not allowed to complain about the chill or the anxiety gnawing away at my spine. If I had been like the others, who were selected and yanked from the protective arms of their loving families, I might have earned the right.

But I volunteered.

The night before I was supposed to leave, I woke up with Celia, my fiancée, chaining my arms to the bed. Her vibrant red hair was pulled back into a thick braid, and her golden, hazel eyes shone with determination.

"I'm tired of losing so much to this curse," she said. "We always send our men. Maybe it's time one of us women take it on, Will. I love you. I'm not losing you to that beast."

I could do nothing but scream into the gag in my mouth as I watched her walk out of my room, headed straight for her death. My guard—one advantage of being the Duke's son—found me the next morning. "She told me if she didn't return, to let you out," he said with an apologetic grimace, prying the gag from between my teeth.

The castle released the first girl, taking Celia in her place. Two nights later, another was stolen from her bed, and none of us knew why. Punishing us for not sending one of our boys like always? Why would Celia's sacrifice equal less? Because she did so to save *me* and not the girl taken?

My knees buckle, and I nearly fall to the snow, my vision suddenly flooded by memories of my sister, the beast's latest victim.

Maris. Maris needs me.

Her laughter rings in my ear. The picture of her long golden hair threaded with flowers on the eve of her sixteenth birthday spurs me forward.

Why another girl?

The council met after my sister was taken. Celia's sacrifice hadn't worked, and they had to decide whether or not letting me volunteer still even mattered.

"We could always send the old witch," one of the council members said when I demanded they allow me to still go to the castle even though Celia had left in my place. Winter was already sharp in the air, the icy chill settling in everyone's bones. "Maybe then the monster would stop claiming our sons and daughters every year."

"Miss Gardner has nothing to do with it," Father insisted, calming them with his measured words and easy demeanor. "My son will fulfill his duty, and he will come out with his life."

His words emboldened the council to accept my proposal to still go to the castle in the woods. I exited my father's office with their eyes on me and the family obligation on my back, every one of us aware Celia's sacrifice wasn't enough to feed the beast.

What would it take next?

The farther I travel into the forest, the harsher winter's thorns dig into my flesh. My knitted cap flies free from my head, and my dark hair tangles in the wind.

"Welcome, lordling."

The feminine voice enters my mind, softer than silk and sharper than the blade in my hand.

Come to save the one you love?

"Get out of my head," I grit out, clenching my eyes closed. Something about the voice is familiar, but I can't place it. It's hidden beneath the gravel and ridges, buried in a valley of secrets.

A laugh rolls in my mind, echoing and biting like the snowy winds sweeping in from the mountains. The winter aches to sink its claws into our village.

I break through the line of trees. The castle looms over me. Vines and thorns snake around the dark gray stone, and poisonous purple flowers flutter in the breeze.

"*No man has lived to tell the tale of my castle, lordling,*" the voice coos.

"Your words have no effect on me."

My father's brother faced the beast and died. My grandfather never allowed him to volunteer, and he carried the weight of cowardice on his shoulders for years. The one year he defied his father, the beast refused him entry, telling him, "*You had many years to defeat me. I will not take your selfish sacrifice.*"

It tells me now, *"Your father inherited this castle, and so will you. He selfishly thought he could claim glory. But a prideful adversary is not better than a fearful one. I'm glad he didn't raise a coward."*

"My father is not a coward!" I shout, releasing my sword from its scabbard. But all I can think of is the look in his eyes when he sent me away at the council meeting: relief. It curls wickedly in my gut.

I force the thought away. My eyes sweep the clearing, but my vision is a prisoner to the shadows from the trees curling around the castle's turrets.

The voice chuckles. *"Even so, I am your past, present, and future. Now I have taken your sister. Nothing you do will thaw the coming winter."*

"Haven't you already taken enough?" I straighten my shoulders, lifting my chin.

Laughter rolls over my skin.

Ice settles in my veins, and I stare up at the castle. The echo in my mind fades, telling me whoever the voice belongs to has slithered back into her cave. The prickling along the back of my neck warns me she isn't far. She wouldn't miss what happens next.

I've been practicing for this moment my entire life, waiting for my name to be called to save the next girl held captive by the beast. Father never stopped training me until I could battle with any blade and could defeat any of his guards.

The year he tried to go, the unforgiving ramifications if the beast is not defeated were the worst the village had ever seen: snowstorms that last for weeks; spoiled food; dwindling resources; neighbors turning against one another; and, eventually, the thing everyone fears . . .

Death.

My feet crunch in the snow and break the silence of the wood. I circle the castle, looking for an opening. Bones splinter beneath my feet. Shock travels through me, and I force back the nausea in my gut. Wind whistles through the trees like the voices of the dead, so fierce and strong that I struggle to find the door. An echoing crack breaks through the howls of an incoming storm. I glance to my right to see a sliver of light passing through a nearly invisible doorway.

I slip inside to escape the wind. The oaken door slams shut behind me. Dimmed torches flicker in the hall.

My heart thunders in my chest, and I grip the hilt of my sword tighter. The hall leads to a wide entryway full of cobwebs and cracked stones.

"Hello?" My voice echoes around me.

A faint strain of music drifts down the wide staircase in the center of the room. I search for the source but come up wanting. The notes mask the whisper of my footsteps as I climb higher, as I twist and turn in the dilapidated halls until I reach an open door in the darkest corner of the castle.

I peer inside, and the air leaves my lungs.

"Maris," I whisper, the word breaking like a promise in my chest.

She hangs suspended by ropes and vines tied to her wrists, black roses vibrantly blooming as their thorns dig into her flesh and draw rivulets of blood. A sphere of transparent golden magic shields her from any aid I can offer. My sister, who would do anything for her family, the one chosen by the beast. But while she can't hold a blade, I grip the pommel of mine tighter.

I run toward her, but I'm thrown back by the shield. I crash into the floor, scattering a cloud of rubble. The voice from before slips into my mind.

"You can't save her," it whispers. The words wrap around me, and I struggle to my feet.

The magic circling my sister pulses like the *buh-duh, buh-duh, buh-duh* of a heartbeat. Her hair hangs limp and greasy, grazing her waist and blowing in a nonexistent breeze. A low humming sounds around the room, overshadowing the music that led me here.

I raise my sword and take a cautious step toward my sister. The shadows meld around me, stretching and reaching for me with delicate, shadowed claws against my exposed skin.

She's bound to the castle, lordling. You'll have to do more than threaten me with a sword.

"Stop hiding in the shadows!" My voice pierces the magic thrumming through the room. The sphere's monotonous hum skips a beat. The shield flickers for half a second.

Maris throws her head back, and a scream rips through her chest. I fight my way to her, slashing at the bonds holding her in the air while the magic stutters. I'm through one vine, Maris's leg dangling limply as a whimper escapes her, when my sword is torn from my hand.

My eyes rake the room, and I stumble back as a woman rises from the shadows. A cloud of mist covers her face, and a hood hides her hair. Darkness drips from her fingertips and weaves in and out of her hood, turning the gloom clouding her face even more menacing.

"Hello, lordling," she says. The voice is unnatural, like stone against stone—beastly, different from the one before.

I unsheath the dagger at my waist and circle her. She breezes around me as shadows fall from her hands and caress my ankles.

"Your move," she whispers.

I lunge at the same time the beast attacks.

She grabs my forearm, throwing me into the nearest wall. Stone breaks free and crashes around me, and I stagger to my feet, my eyes trained on her.

"That's the best you've got?" I ask.

I advance. She grabs me again and wrestles me to the ground. I drive my elbow into her chin. She hisses in pain, releasing her hold. I rush to my feet, and she circles me. What began as a fight turns into a dance.

Finally, she lunges toward me. She blocks each dip I feign. My blade slices the air as she ducks under my arm. Every move I make, she anticipates the next two. So I think three steps ahead. Instead of going under, I go left, my non-dominant side. The blade sinks into her abdomen, and a gasp fills the air. All other sound in the room ceases to exist, and I catch the beast—this woman—as she and the shadows begin to fall. Her hood cascades to her shoulders, revealing a face I only thought I'd see in my dreams.

Hair the color of a burning sunset and eyes sweeter than honey.

"Celia . . ."

"Save her, Will . . ." Celia croaks. "Save her . . . The beast . . . she's too strong. She'll heal me, but . . . she'll kill you both . . ."

"Celia!" My voice scratches its way up my throat. "Celia!"

The ground beneath my feet shakes, and the walls tremble. I spin around in time to see my sister hanging by a single vine, over eight feet off the ground. I lay Celia down and rush over to Maris before she's nothing but a broken doll.

I reach her just in time for her to fall into my arms, knocking us both to the floor.

"Maris?" I tap her cheek and watch the steady rise and fall of her chest.

Her eyelashes flutter at the sound of her name. "Will?"

A cry escapes my lips. "You're alive! But what about Celia—"

Her eyes flash open. "Celia is in danger, Will. She didn't have a choice. The monster took her! She tried to use me, but the curse wouldn't allow it. Two women have never been to the castle at the same time before."

"What does that mean—" I start, but she interrupts me with the only words that could steal my own.

"The monster wants Celia to take *its* place—" A scream breaks from her throat as the cobbles shift beneath us. The floor threatens to open beneath us and silence her.

"We need to leave." I glance back at where I left the woman I love, only to see a trail of blood leading into the shadows.

The soft caress of Celia's voice enters my mind, and I wonder how long it will take before it becomes unrecognizable and beastly.

Leave, Will . . . and don't come back! Celia's voice ends in a hiss, and then her scream echoes between my ears.

I grit my teeth against the sound, and it's a few moments before I realize Maris is shaking me. "Will, we have to leave!"

Maris struggles to her feet, and I stumble to mine. We rush through the castle, leaving half my soul in the ruined bricks as it falls apart around us. Large oaken door blocks the exit, but it's thrown open by an invisible force. Outstretched limbs from the forest beyond welcome us. Broken branches and slush crunch beneath our feet. The ground rumbles, letting us only move as fast as our wounds allow. Sharp winds howl; freezing rain slices through the air. Finally, the village lights appear.

Maris slumps against me, and I swing her into my arms. Covered in mud and soaked through with blood and rain, I crash into the tavern door.

"Open up!" I pound my fist into the door. "Maris," I whisper. "Stay awake, Maris."

The door opens, and we fall into the heat and eerie quiet. I can barely make out the villagers piled inside because of the blood and water in my eyes.

"Help her," I say before crumbling to the ground and welcoming the silence.

I jerk upright at the sound of a teapot's whistle.

"Whoa there, young man," says a croaking voice.

I look over to the woman sitting beside me, recognizing her. A white rose, half hidden by her ashen hair, dangles behind her ear. Candlelight flickers off the emerald stem and thin petals as she shifts beside my bed—how did I end up in a bed?

"Where am I? Where's Maris—"

"She's at home, safe and sound," Mistress Gardner says. "Didn't expect to wake up with the village pariah tending to you, much less in her humble cottage?"

I rush to my feet, but a wave of dizziness overcomes me.

"Sit." An invisible hand forces me down.

I search for something to say, but she snaps her fingers, and the words stick in my throat. While everyone calls her a witch, I've never seen her power. I didn't realize I only half believed the rumors until I see it before my eyes.

"Don't wear yourself down." She stands and pours a cup of tea. "And, yes, I am a witch. Drink this, and then we can talk."

She hands me the tea. For a brief moment, I consider dumping out its contents. She trains her eyes on me until I hesitantly bring it to my lips and take a sip. A flood of warmth spreads through my body, the ache in my bones disappearing.

After I finish it, she stands and shuffles to the other side of the room. I can barely make out her form in the muted light.

"Why am I in your cottage and not my parents' home?"

"There's something you need to understand."

But I don't want to understand. I want answers.

The hair on the back of my neck rises, and I slide closer to the end of the bed, the door within reach.

"I wouldn't do that, Lord William," she says, voice low. "Keeping you here wasn't my idea, only my kindness." She snaps her fingers, and the candles around the room flare to life. Herbs and cloudy containers cover all available surfaces, and the crisp smell of spring hangs in the air like a reprieve from the harsh winter.

"Is my sister here, too?"

Mistress Gardner shakes her head.

"Why send my sister home and me here? How is she any safer than I am? I didn't—" The words stick in my throat. "I didn't . . . kill the beast."

"Your sister is safe. Your parents don't want you to return to the beast's castle, so they thought it was best to place you here, where I could keep an eye on you."

"My mother, you mean?"

She smiles. "Men often forget that behind them stands a strong woman. That same woman can also play her hand when the time strikes. Your mother showed her cards."

My hands tighten into fists, and I turn all my fury on Mistress Gardner. "You expect me to believe my mother trusted you?"

"Your father may control the council, but he does not share all their ideas." She studies me for a moment. "You stumbled into that tavern, half-crazed and bleeding. They were concerned about your physical ailments, but your mental struggles worried them even more. It took them days to wake you and your sister, and the entire time you were mumbling about Celia."

"Because she's alive! She barely had control over herself. That . . . *thing* is inside her!"

"I know."

I swallow. "What do you need me to understand?"

She harrumphs. "I never expected my mother's magic to travel this far."

My brow furrows.

She continues, "My mother was the witch who cursed this town, and I've been waiting for someone like you to break the curse since the day she died. She made sure my magic alone wasn't strong enough."

Heat rises in my cheeks. Mistress Gardner was an old woman when my father was a boy—when his father was barely a man at seventeen. Her unexplainable age and her home covered in white roses at the edge of the forest are partly to blame for the villagers' hatred. Even when our crops fail or our supplies mysteriously spoil midwinter, her white roses continue to bloom in the roughest conditions.

"I'm older than I look, and so is this curse." She takes the rose from her hair and twirls it between her fingers. "Your great-great-grandmother brought it to this village when she came to my mother and demanded a daughter as innocent as freshly fallen snow and as beautiful as a rose, someone to be hers and hers alone. Your great-great-grandfather was a cruel man and taught his boys the same acts of cruelty. But roses have their thorns, and while your great-aunt was the most beautiful woman this village—maybe even the kingdom—had ever seen, she was the most dangerous. Rhoswen was still her father's daughter."

I shake my head. "My father has taken responsibility for the curse—and my grandfather before him."

She smiles, holding out the rose. "Then watch and see the truth of what happened that fateful day, William. To get to the end, you have to understand the beginning."

I take the rose from her, and a thorn pricks my finger. Wincing, I watch the ruby-red drop splash on the cobblestone floor before I'm looking up into a new world.

I'm standing in a memory of the castle, the edges of it frayed. Instead of the dilapidated ruins that held my sister prisoner, the setting sun streaks liquid gold through the stained glass windows and across the floor. The smells of fresh roses and lavender assault my senses. Rich, plush carpets muffle incoming footsteps.

"Rhoswen!" The female voice echoes from downstairs, and I step out of the way as a girl about my age storms down the steps in a dress of pure white except for the splattering of red on her corset. Even with her gruesome appearance from the red splattering on her torso, the sun seems to follow her around the room, shining bronze light haloing her head. But with the light, shadows dance from every place she touches.

A woman chases after her, brown hair flying behind her. She grabs Rhoswen's arm and yanks her back before her fingers can graze the front door. "How could you be so reckless?" the woman demands.

A mirthless laugh escapes the girl's lips. "I hurt no one, not physically anyway. Besides, Julia Gardner is nothing more than the local witch's daughter. What's a little paint? You're acting as if I killed her, Mother."

"Did you see her? And to bring those *friends* of yours in on it."

Rhoswen's face doesn't change. She rips her hand from her mother's grasp and straightens her dress.

The doors to the castle fly open, slamming into her mother and tossing her like a rag doll. Rhoswen rushes to her side. "Mother!"

A figure clad in shadows crosses the threshold and throws Rhoswen against the wall. She crumples to the ground in a heap of white.

"Who are you?" Rhoswen croaks. Her fierceness remains in the strong set of her shoulders and clenched jaw. Her eyes narrow as she stands, but an invisible force pulls her back down.

The figure lowers her hood to reveal pale white hair and a red smile. "The village always calls me a witch, so I thought it was time I show you what I can do."

"What do you want?" Rhoswen asks.

"To make you as ugly on the outside as you are on the inside. That *witch* was my daughter."

The fight in Rhoswen is gone, and she stands as if in a trance. The witch's lips twitch in a smile. "This place will become your prison. When your body dies, your mind will live on. The village will suffer for the blind eye they turned toward your cruelty, losing both their girls and boys until someone worthy can rescue a victim of this curse and *defeat* you." She produces a flower from the folds of her cloak: a rose as white as snow. "This rose will never lose its bloom until that person comes to destroy it."

The world spins around me, and I drop my white rose as I return to the present. Mistress Gardner waits on the other side of the vision, catching me as I fall near the bed.

"I was a teenager then, the same age as Rhoswen," she says. "My mother wasn't well-liked, but I had made a few friends. I was beautiful in my own way, confident with my looks, while fragile when it came to friendships. Rhoswen was threatened by me for some reason or another, whether because of my looks or the tenuous hold I had on the few villagers I befriended.

"I had elementary magic back then. One of the girls in on the prank was a friend, supposedly.

They wanted to humiliate me, push me into the river and force me to walk home in the snow, dripping wet and shivering. It was the coldest winter this village had ever seen, but it still wasn't enough for Rhoswen. With some help, she took it even farther and gave me this scar." She pulls back her hair and shows the puckered pink line traveling from her temple to her chin.

"Until your Celia, only men came to the castle. My mother wanted the town to suffer the loss of the men who had held me while Rhoswen attacked and the ones who would follow. After taking their future, she took their memories of the incident. She wanted this place to relearn their actions, but I doubt she imagined it would outlast her. When Celia decided to face the beast herself, Rhoswen saw her chance. She was able to free part of her soul and trap Celia's as the guardian of the castle, controlling her while they both remain locked inside."

Mistress Gardner stares at her hands, her brow furrowing. "For a long time, I was angry at my mother for isolating us even further from the town. But she hadn't, not really. The damage had been done by small-mindedness. She only brought it to the light."

I shake my head. "How did I make it out alive?"

She smiles. "Because you did not travel to the castle to gain glory but to right a wrong. Selfishness and pride, which drove Rhoswen when she cursed her family and this place with her choices, are the ugliest things of all. There's still time to save Celia, but you'll have to be smart about it."

"How am I supposed to do that?" I throw out my hands, hoping she'll toss me the answer.

"Take these with you." Mistress Gardner reaches behind her, producing a longsword and a dagger. A faint light of enchantment emanates from them. "You have to defeat the beast and save yourself from a bitter winter by breaking the curse. My mother wasn't without her faults, but she would never create an unbreakable curse. The only reason I can talk about it now is because someone *finally* volunteered."

"All these years. . ."

Mistress Gardner nods. "She gave these weapons to me, but no one has been ready until you. I tried to break the curse myself, but Mother put up strongholds against that. She thought she was doing me a favor, and the blades wouldn't work for me. They shone for the first time when you volunteered. When a worthy opponent wields these blades, they can break any enchantment. You were gone before I could catch you last time." She winks, and I think there are some things—like how this curse hasn't made her bitter—about this woman I will never understand.

I slide the blades into their sheaths.

"Aim true, and they will never fail you." She walks to the door, unlocks it and slides out. The door's key rests on a nearby table, shining gold in the candlelight. She tosses me a smile before I escape into the falling snow. "Choose well, young lordling. You may have magic on your side, but you must also fight it."

I rush through the snow back to my family's manor. Before I go, I have to see my sister—to at least know she's protected and healing. If the task of defeating the beast is as difficult as the witch promises, even with blessed blades, this could be the last time I speak with her.

A loud hum echoes from the center of the village as I pass through. As the sun begins its descent below the horizon, the sky blazes with torchlight. Voices carry above the buildings that line the streets.

Unease settles in my stomach, but I swallow the sourness rising in my throat and sprint back to my family's home. I sneak in through an opening in the boundary wall, a place only my father and I know about, and slip through the kitchens.

Compared to outside, an eerie silence hangs over the manor. I rush to the nearest window and catch flickers of movement in the dark where the few guards patrol our property. I duck down with the hope of not being seen.

The sun has almost disappeared below the horizon when I make it upstairs. I make for the servants' hall instead of the main staircase and find my sister's room heavily guarded.

"What are you doing?" a high, elegant voice asks behind me, its owner privy to my hiding spot in the shadows.

I freeze. *Mother.* "I—I was checking on Maris."

She grabs my wrist and pulls me into an empty room. "What are you doing here, Will?"

"I came to see Maris."

Mother touches my cheek. Her hair hangs over her shoulders in limp waves of gold. "I asked Mistress Gardner to watch after you. Why aren't you resting—"

"I have to save Celia," I interrupt.

"No, you do not." Her voice is sharp, cold. She wrenches her hand away. "You need to go back to the cottage where you're safe like *she* promised. It's the only way to keep you safe. The castle is still . . . *alive*." She chokes on the word, and I wrap her in my arms.

"What happened?"

"It's not natural, neither the castle nor what it does to this place when winter comes," she says into my shoulder, but I can't tell if she's speaking to me or through me. "You weren't supposed to live. I mourned you *both*. I can't lose you again." She pulls back and implores me with her gaze. Her fingers dig into my arms. Her nails threaten to tear the fabric of my doublet. "You don't have to go back to the witch, but I didn't know what else to do to keep you away from this—"

I cup her face in my hands. "I have to save Celia," I whisper. "I love her. I'm going to marry her. This is about our *family*, and she is part of that."

She shakes her head. "She will be the death of you."

The words sharpen my resolve and steel my heart. "Not doing anything when there's a chance would be my demise. Please, Mother."

She touches my cheek. "Is there any way to talk you out of it?"

I shake my head. "Let me go."

The door behind her creaks open, and I meet my father's eyes, a bronzed mirror of my own. "Let him go, Lorcella."

Mother spins around, the dissent blooming on her lips. She tenses at the look in his eye, and her head bows. She turns back to me and cups my cheek. Her thumb rubs over the small scrape near my chin. Finally, she nods.

"Thank you," I say, kissing her forehead. "I will return. I promise."

She smiles with tears shining in her eyes. "Be safe." She turns away as if unable to watch me go.

The guards don't stop me as I walk into my sister's room. My mother hovers in the hall. Maris's hair is a fan around her head as her chest rises and falls with each intake of breath.

I lean over her and touch an infinitesimal cut on her forehead, a scab already starting to form. "At least you're safe," I mumble.

Without waking her, I tuck a strand of hair behind her ear and escape back into the hall, intent on saving another piece of my heart.

The villagers are hysterical, and fire and swords cover the town square as one of the merchants demands vengeance for the decades of suffering. They've snapped under the pressure of having lost another girl to the curse before the first one was even rescued, and they fear losing more before the beast is satisfied. The still-deepening winter has sent them to the precipice.

I cover my face with the hood of my cloak and slip through the crowd. Frenzied by their anger, no one notices as I disappear into the forest. My lungs ache with each intake of icy air as the winter barrels ahead. The castle is fighting back, ready to claim the next girl to keep the curse active. It needs a life to fuel the enchantment, and it needs a hero to sacrifice himself to save the girl.

I step into the courtyard, and the ground shifts beneath my feet.

"*Welcome back, lordling,*" the voice whispers in my ear. "*Have you come to save another?*" An echo of a smile at the end of her words is sharper than the sword at my waist.

A grimace works onto my lips as snow and ice fill the air. "When I do free her, what becomes of you?"

The temperature around me plummets.

"*Do not speak of what you do not understand, William Rhodes. We come from the same vine, nephew. It's difficult to get rid of the root without destroying the shoot.*"

Silence settles over the courtyard, and the little warmth available to me rises back in my cheeks. I unsheath my sword and take a step toward the front door, glancing back and searching for signs of the villagers.

Before my hand can wrap around the iron handle, the double doors to the castle creak open.

"Celia?" I whisper into the crumbling space.

My footsteps echo on the cracked floor, clouds forming in front of my face with each breath. Flickers of candlelight illuminate the room and create shadowy figures that move with me.

As soon as I'm through the doors, they slam shut behind me. The lock slides into place.

The voice's eagerness spreads through me and raises the hair on the back of my neck. "*I see you came back to play, little lordling.*"

"You want a game? Test me, Rhoswen. Give me your best because I can take anything you throw at me." My words bounce against the stone walls. "To me, this is life or death, and I think you feel the same. I win, you release Celia."

"*Celia will be your prize. Destroy the heart of the flower in the tower, and she'll be yours. Two souls will leave this place, forever. I promise.*"

"If you win—"

"*You presume to understand what I want, lordling. Am I not allowed to name my own prize?*"

Goosebumps pepper my flesh. The words trace my skin, a snake slithering beneath my clothes. "What is it you want?"

"*To be truly rid of this prison, to not die inside it. Free me.*"

I push back the lump in my throat. "How do I free you?"

"*In order to be free from this curse, a willing vessel has to take my place.*"

"That's why you're still here, even with Celia. She's not a willing vessel."

She remains silent, but I feel her hovering in the corners of my mind. Finally she asks, "*Do we have a deal, lordling?*"

If she wins, Celia and I both die. It would be a worse death to know I tried and wasn't able to save her. "Yes," rises to my lips.

"*Then let the games begin. I pray you can make it to her tower.*"

A fierce wind blows through the entryway, snuffing out the candles and robbing the room of light. The castle settles around me like a lion settling on its haunches before pouncing, and a slithering sound resounds in the room.

"I told you not to come back," a gravelly voice says. "You were supposed to take her and run."

"Celia? Celia, let me help you—"

I'm knocked to the ground. The air rushes from my lungs, and my no longer illuminated blade flies from my hand, skittering farther into the darkness.

"You can't fight this," she says. "You can't fight *her*."

The slithering hiss rises in my ears and wraps around my throat. I reach for the thing holding me to the ground, but my fingers pass through smoke. My body spasms, begging for air, and I force my muscles to relax and my brain to *think*.

I fumble for the dagger at my waist and slash at the invisible creature holding me down. A screech fills the chamber, and the candles relight with orange and blue flames. I roll onto my side, gulping in lungfuls of air.

I take in the room around me. Thorn-covered vines slink over the floors and up the walls, racing toward me. I slice at them with my dagger, and the blade turns the golden hue of the sun. Pain lances behind my eyes; I have to squint against the sudden brightness. A shriek erupts from the plant, and the exposed root and vine shrivel before exploding in a puff of smoke.

I lunge for my sword, but one of the vines grabs my back foot. I slash at it with my dagger, and its piercing scream rings in my ears. My fingers fumble for my sword, which is almost in reach, before another vine grabs the blade and throws it across the room.

A scream rips from my throat, and I slash through the next vine trying to grab me. I sprint for the sword and clasp the hilt before the vine latches on. Light pierces the room as my hand meets the blade, and the insidious plant shrivels before it bursts into dust. The debris settles in the air, touching my skin and clogging my lungs, but I push past the discomfort and storm upstairs.

A faint glow streams from the next level, and my eyes train on it. Wind whistles through the cracks in the castle, and I almost don't see the beasts until they're on me.

Three wolves launch at me from the shadows, and I swing my sword wide. One of them catches the brunt of my blade and lands in a whimpering heap at the bottom of the stairs. The other two dash forward, lips pulled back in snarls.

One ducks away from my swinging blade as the other pounces. It latches onto my arm and rips through fabric and skin, drawing blood. A hiss escapes my lips, and fear threatens to weaken my resolve. Adrenaline pushes through the sharp pain and intense emotions warring inside me, and I'm able to slice at it. My blow lands true, and a huge gash appears on its shoulder. It howls in agony and disappears into the shadows. The other lifts its maw, crying out in anguish.

When it comes for me, I'm ready.

We circle each other, one of my eyes trained on the faint glow coming from the next level and the other on the gray wolf. Saliva drips from its teeth and pools on the floor.

"Come on!" I scream.

It pounces.

I dart out of its path and bring up my sword. The blade sinks into the wolf's belly, and it falls to the ground with the cry of death. I rise to my feet, staring at the remains of my battle. The chest of one of the wolves rises and falls unsteadily, but I leave it, hoping that once I break this curse, whatever holds it here will break, too.

I limp up the stairs, holding my arm to my chest and the sword in my other hand. Debris, broken glass, and remains of a life once lived litter the path to the double doors at the end of the hall.

My footsteps slow the closer I get to the light, and I glance around, trying to locate shadows of things waiting to jump out. A door waits at the end of the hall. The wood is cool against my fingers as I press my way into the room. I'm frozen by the sight in front of me.

My eyes barely register the pulsating rose at the top of the tower, the shining flower rising from the center of the room and hovering waist-high. But my attention is drawn elsewhere—on the two girls standing behind it.

"Maris, what are you doing?" I ask, the words barely a whisper. How had she snuck out of the manor?

"What you don't have the power to do," my sister says, the blade in her hand under Celia's throat. A trickle of blood seeps into the neck of Celia's white dress, tangling with her russet curls.

"Hello, William," Celia whispers, fully herself instead of half-hidden by the monster. Her sad smile stops my heart; I ache to rush to her, kiss the salted tears from her cheeks, and envelop her in my arms.

"Celia." My eyes flash to my sister. "How did you get past the guards?" *Why* had she snuck past the guards? Unease settles in my bones, and the adrenaline that got me through the wolves begins to claw its way up my throat.

Maris snorts. Her casualty hits worse than a blow. "I told Mother I needed rest. Alone. Then I used the same secret places you used to sneak through when we were children. You thought you and Father were the only ones who knew about those?"

My eyes flash to Celia. I want to give her all the words I never thought I'd be able to say, but I bottle them inside and turn toward my sister. "Let her go, Maris. We can end this. We can free her—"

"You don't understand! She's in my head! I had to come—this is the only way!" Anger colors Maris's cheeks; tears and snot cover her face. "You weren't held prisoner here. This is the only way! We have to kill the thing that keeps the castle alive."

I lay my sword down. "That's not Celia. Can't you feel it? There's someone else here. *That's* who we have to destroy, and the only way to do that is to free Celia. If she doesn't have a vessel, then she can't thrive. We can destroy it from the root!"

"There's no destroying it. I've tried! That's why I followed you. Don't you see? She *is* the root. Celia is connected to it. There was only ever one way to end this." She grabs Celia's wrist and shoves it forward. Roots anchored to the castle disappear into Celia's skin, pulsating with their own heartbeat.

I clench my jaw and move toward her. "There is a way, Maris. Put the knife down. Please."

"I can't. I'm sorry."

I hold out my dagger at the same moment Maris begins to slide the knife over Celia's throat. My blade makes impact before my sister can finish her motion, and a scream pierces the air as the blade buries into the flesh of her hand. The knife slides across the floor, half hidden in the shadows. She drops Celia, and I move my fiancée behind me, though it's difficult with the roots still bursting from her flesh. "Will—" Celia begins.

"Why would you do that? There was a chance to break this curse!" Maris glares at me, hot tears pouring down her cheeks. "Now we're doomed to forever repeat it because you can't give her up. She needs a willing sacrifice!"

"Will, listen to me," Celia tries to say, but I break away from her and step toward my sister.

"I didn't want to hurt you, Maris, but you don't understand."

My sister yanks the blade out of her hand, her knees hitting the ground with a hard crack. I rush toward her, but I'm wrenched backward. Thorns dig into my arms, and I'm spun to face the girl I love.

"You should have let me go," Celia whispers, holding onto the vines jutting from her wrists. "Maris understands. She's had her *in her head*. You can't save us all. It would have been kinder for you to kill me."

"I can't do that, Celia." I grab onto the vines to pull her closer.

"Stop! Take Maris and *leave,*" Celia says. "Never come back here! I will take her place. I will take Rhoswen's place. The rose's petals have already started to fall." I glance at the flower in the center of the room. It blooms a brilliant white on top of a crumbling dias. Petals litter the floor at the base of stone. Another falls as I study it. "The winter won't last long," she promises.

"The winter always returns." I tug hard on the vines, gritting my teeth against the sharp pain in my arms that has not grabbed onto my legs and torso. "You will die here, and then what? What happens when you die?"

She smiles. Her tears flash in the light from the rose still hovering between us. "I won't die. I'll be here until the end of time, keeping the village safe. No girls will be taken, never again."

"But you will die." I wrench her another step closer, then one more. "You will die every day you spend here alone. Time will cease to matter, and you will be no more because this place will kill your soul." We're so close now that I can feel the beat of her heart, the beat of the vines, against my chest. "And I will not leave you here to die. I won't. I refuse to leave you."

I release my hold on the vines and grab the dagger at my waist. My hand wraps around the hilt as I'm yanked back and thrown into the nearest wall. I slice the blade out in front of me, and the vines let go.

A piercing scream echoes in the room as the plants shrivel and die in puffs of dust. Celia falls to the ground with a cry. Two of the women I care for most lie on either side of the rose as I pierce it with my blade and release the blinding light of the sun.

Every shadow ceases to exist as the ground shudders beneath my feet. I release the blade, and the weight of endless winters drops from my shoulders.

I leave the dagger and dash toward my sister. "Maris, you've got to wake up!"

"Will?" she whispers, waking only partially. "What—how—"

"Stand up, Maris, and get out of here! This place is about to fall." My sister nods and starts to push herself up.

I leave her as she rises to her feet and head toward Celia. Blood courses from her wrists and pools on the floor. I rip off my doublet and yank it apart, tying the strips around her wrists to stop the flow. Anxiety cripples my usually steady movements.

"Leave me, Will—"

I capture her face in my hands. My heart races in my chest and it forces the words from my lips.

"There is nothing—*nothing*—in this world or the next that would make me leave you." I pull her close and place my mouth on hers, trying to convey every missed moment, forgotten touch, and unspoken word in a single kiss.

Her lips move against mine, quick and fierce, and I pull away and cradle her in my arms.

I search for my sister and find her hovering in the doorway, breathing heavily through her nose. The ground shakes once, twice, three times, and I run for the exit with Celia in my arms. Urgency clogs my throat, and I force myself to ask Maris, "You good?"

She nods stiffly. "Just my hand." She angles her gaze toward her fist, blood seeping between her fingers.

"Follow me and don't look back."

We race through the castle, and the heavy weight in my chest starts to lift the closer we get to the entrance. The outside shines brightly with the torchlight of the villagers as they arrive from the forest, but the doors slam shut when we're inches away.

Not so fast, lordling, the voice says, the pain evident in her words. *You . . . must . . . end this.*

"What more do you want?" I spin in circles, cradling Celia to my chest. "I destroyed the rose! This castle is coming down—"

"*You must choose . . . you agreed only two souls would leave this place. You're . . . demanding three.*"

"You lured my sister here!" I scream. "She has already been rescued—"

Choose . . .

The castle begins to collapse around us, and I run over to Maris. "Can you carry her, at least over the threshold?"

"William, you can't—" Maris says.

Celia's eyes do not open as I press my lips against her temple. I look back to my sister. "Can you do it?"

Maris blinks back her tears and manages one stiff nod. "I can."

I give Celia to Maris. She strains against her weight, and I reach for the handle.

"I'm sorry," Maris whispers. "I'm so—"

I lean over and cup her cheek. "I love you, Mari. Now, go." The doors magically swing open. I watch my sister and the girl I love fall into the waiting crowd. The doors to the castle slam shut behind them, and I spin to face the voice. A woman, a little older than the Rhoswen from the memo-ry, staggers into the entryway. The remains of the building collapse all around her.

"Have you come to take my place?" she asks, the sound no longer in my mind yet still sharp and sure.

"If that's what I must do, then I will gladly take your place if it saves them."

She slouches on the ground in a mess of black fabric and pain. Her hood falls away, revealing a pale, weary countenance and aged eyes. "Then come end it, William Rhodes. End my suffering."

I lower myself in front of her, and she takes her hands in mine. They're surprisingly warm. She smiles up at me. "Thank you," she whispers before kissing my cheek.

Sound ceases, and I'm left surrounded by dark-ness, peace, and the flicker of a smile not my own.

I wake with a start, not sure where I am.

"Hello, William Rhodes."

I jerk upright and glance to my left to see Mistress Gardner sitting beside me on the grass. "What happened? Where am I?"

"You broke the curse," she says, not looking at me but gazing at the stars. "We're in the in-between place." The stars take on a life of their own, dancing in the rushing dawn. I close my eyes and shake away the unsettling, dizzy feeling it gives me.

I glance around. Instead of trees and a crumbling castle, I'm in the soft grasses of a meadow. Wildflowers pepper the valley, and mountains rise in the distance. "Is this my prison? Somewhere in between real life and the curse?"

A laugh rolls from her lips. "No, William. I have come to offer you a choice."

I shake my head. "What kind of choice? I'm done making deals—"

She raises her hand. "This isn't a deal. This is a gift. I have lived more years than some can fathom and seen more things than others can dream up. Your life has barely begun. I wish to take your place. Your life would still be a cursed one since you took Rhoswen's place, but not with my sacrifice. You chose to save the girl you loved, but I am choosing to end this."

"I don't understand." I rest my chin on my forearms. "How does your sacrifice end this? I'm a willing vessel for the curse—"

"Your soul would be trapped here, in this place," she says with a shake of her head. Her gaze remains fixed on a point beyond the mountains. "What I'm offering you is an end to it. A true break, something only I can give you. I couldn't before, not without your sacrifice. My life is over, William. It has been for a long time. This is my gift to you, my life for yours. All I'm asking is for you to let me end it in the way I want."

"But—are you sure?"

"This is what I want," she says, still not looking at me. "It's my time to leave. Do you accept the trade?" Finally, her gaze meets mine, and I see hope mingled with a great weariness.

"Yes," I say, the word a breath between my lips.

Mistress Gardner turns her head to the sky and disappears into the night, a sigh of relief flowing past her lips. The world snaps into focus. A delicate breeze dances over my skin as I step back into the winter. Its harshness isn't bitter over my flesh but welcome—hopeful.

I rush down the broken steps of the castle to Celia and Maris and fall down beside them, pulling them into a tight embrace. The villagers watch our reunion in silence. The light from their torches flickers in and out of existence. An audible gasp fills the quiet, and I turn. Behind me, the castle rebuilds itself into its original state, grand arches and towering trellises rising above the snow-laden trees.

Celia's eyes widen in shock. "The castle...it's..."

Maris looks back and barks out a laugh. "You broke the curse." She buries me in another unrelenting hug and whispers in my ear, "Don't you *ever* do that again."

"You've exceeded your limit on bad decisions for the rest of your life," Celia says, when my sister finally lets go. She cups my cheek and gives me a watery smile.

I plant a kiss on her forehead and breathe in the peaceful smells of lavender and frost. "Sacrificing myself for you would have been the best decision I ever made."

Celia's tears finally fall. "I love you so much, William Rhodes," she says and pulls me in for a kiss.

"The curse is broken." Mother pushes through the crowd. The fear I saw on her face the last time we spoke is replaced with relief. She falls to her knees in the snow with tears rolling down her cheeks and laughter falling from her lips. Maris rushes over to her and hugs her even tighter than she had me. Mother's eyes never leave me, unlike the villagers who stare in shock at the scene shifting before them.

She pulls herself and Maris up and walks over to Celia and me. "Let's go home." She helps us to our feet and leads us back toward the village. "This castle needs to rest as much as we do. It's time for a . . . beautiful winter."

The rest of the villagers follow us back through the rising dawn, their blades sheathed and a lightness in the air as snow falls onto the path. Winter continues without its thorns, and the sun blossoms like a rose over the mountains as we make our way home.

Acknowledgements

Every story I write is a blessing from the masterful storyteller. It's in His image I can create one adventure after the other, and I'm forever grateful to my Savior, Jesus Christ, for His endless love.

This story first appeared in the anthology *Sharper Than Thorns*. It was the first time I saw my words in a physical book, and it will forever hold a special place in my heart. Since then, it's been revised and edited. Thank you to my publisher, Twenty Hills, for believing in my wild ideas. You make my stories all the better.

To my editors, Anne and Beka, thank you for finding the nitpickiest things to fix about Will's journey.

Also, to my mom, dad, mother-in-law, and father-in-law, thank you for never hesitating to buy whichever story I have out next in the world.

To my brother, for forgiving me for forgetting to include you in the acknowledgements in my debut novel. I dedicated this one to you!

My grandmother passed before she got to hold this story by itself, but she read it in its original form in *Sharper Than Thorns*. Even though you're in a better place, I wish you could have a chance to reread it. You read this story to Papa, and I'm thankful he'll have it reread to him, even if not by you. *Thorns of Winter* is a story of family, most of all. There is a missing piece in ours without you here.

To my husband: you never hesitate to let me spend all my free time coming up with endless story ideas. Without your support, I wouldn't be able to follow this dream. I love you!

Lastly, to all my readers, being an author wouldn't be nearly as fun without people to share the stories with. Thank you for loving every character and adventure. You make this dream possible!

Moriah is the author of the 3-times Realm Makers finalist young adult fantasy, *Heart of the Sea,* and various short stories. Her next novel, a YA speculative mystery, is coming from Twenty Hills Publishers September 2025. She is a two-time graduate from the University of South Carolina with a Bachelor's in Liberal Arts and a Master's in Library and Information Science. It's been said you can find her perusing bookstores, attempting to persuade strangers to read her favorite books, oscillating between watching the *Lord of*

the Rings trilogy (her husband's favorite) or *Harry Potter* (hers), and keeping her books from the clutches of her two feisty cats.

9 781956 499339